the CLeo stories

The Necklace
and
The Present

For Freya, Ivy, Amy,
Jo and Jess ~ L.G.

For Libby and Ivy ~ F.B.

the CLeo stories

The Necklace *and* The Present

Libby Gleeson
Freya Blackwood

ALLEN&UNWIN
SYDNEY · MELBOURNE · AUCKLAND · LONDON

Cleo

and the necklace

Red, blue, green, yellow, orange and black.
Cleo McCann is making a birthday card for Nick.
It's his party this afternoon.
Everyone will be there.

Cleo draws a '6'. Balloons and gold stars fill the page. She writes: 'Happy Birthday, Nick. From Cleo.' Mum has written it for her on a bit of paper.

'Fabulous,' says Uncle Tom. 'You're a real artist.' He helps her fold the paper to make a card. The '6' is at the front.

After lunch it's time to get ready.

'Why don't you wear this?' says Mum. 'It's perfect for summer.'

She holds up a dress. It's yellow like the sand and blue like the waves.

'No,' says Cleo. 'I'm wearing my Christmas T-shirt that Grandma gave me.'

'But it's not Christmas and you'll be too hot.'

'I don't care.'

Cleo puts on her red T-shirt with the Christmas tree on it. Then she looks in her dress-up box for her spotty shorts. She picks up the present for Nick. 'I'm ready,' she says.

Mum says nothing.

At the party, Isabella is showing Nick her card.

'Listen,' she says. 'Push the button
and it plays Happy Birthday.'

Everyone wants to have a turn. Cleo's card
lies on the table with all the presents.

They play pass the parcel and pin the tail on
the donkey. Cleo pins it on the donkey's left ear.

Everyone laughs. After a moment
Cleo laughs too.

Then they play hide-and-seek. Cleo hides under
Nick's bed with Isabella and Sophie. It's hot and
stuffy but they lie there, whispering. 'See my new
necklace,' says Isabella. 'I got this for Christmas
from my nonna.'

She lets Sophie touch the necklace.
'My nonna says it has real diamonds.'

'I've got a necklace too,' says Sophie.
'Look, mine has precious jewels and it's
gold and I got a matching bangle.'

Cleo is about to say that she got her T-shirt for Christmas and the whole family came, even Uncle Tom from America, and now he's going to stay here. They all went to the beach for dinner and a swim. She is suddenly quiet. Maybe the other girls will think a T-shirt is not such a great present, not like a necklace. She touches her bare neck. What would a necklace feel like?

Footsteps come into the room. The girls put their hands over their mouths and lie very still.

They hear someone opening the cupboard door. Then a voice says, 'There's no one here.'

Isabella giggles.

Nick and Dylan look under the bed.

'Gotcha! Time for birthday cake,' they say.

First they have tiny pink sausages with tomato sauce, carrot sticks and slices of cheese. Then they have baby cupcakes with thick chocolate icing and mini ice-cream cones. Isabella and Sophie show everyone their necklaces.

'I've got one too,' says Mia. 'It's got a gold chain and pink stones but I left it at home.'

'Ta da!' Nick's dad turns off the lights. Nick's birthday cake shines in the dark. It's green like a soccer field with white icing lines on the pitch and tiny teddies playing with a lollipop ball. Six candles are alight along the edges. Nick takes the biggest breath in the world and blows out the candles in one go.

The lights snap back on. Everyone claps and sings, 'Happy birthday to you.' The cake is delicious.

Yum. Yum. Yum.

'Would you like some more?' says Nick's dad.

Cleo shakes her head and rubs her tummy.
'I'm full,' she says.

When it's time to go home everyone gets a party bag
with lollies and a special treat inside. Cleo crosses
her fingers for luck. Maybe she will get a necklace.

Out of her bag falls a
plastic trumpet.
She puts it to
her lips and
blows but
no sound
comes out.

When Cleo goes home, she is so tired that she flops on the lounge-room couch. Her eyes close.

'That must have been a great party,' says Dad as he carries her up to bed.

'I need a necklace,' she says.

'Let's talk about it in the morning,' he says as he tucks her in.

She lies under the fan and dreams of playing soccer in her Christmas T-shirt.

Everyone else in her team is wearing a necklace. Diamonds and coloured jewels sparkle in the sunshine.

The next morning at breakfast Cleo says, 'I have to get a necklace.'

'Have to?' says Mum. 'Why?'

'Because.'

'Because why?'

'Everyone's got a necklace.'

'Who is everyone?'

'Isabella and Sophie and Mia.'

Dad stops stirring his coffee. He looks at Mum. She shrugs her shoulders.

'Three friends does not mean everyone,' Dad says. 'Do you really want one?'

Cleo nods as she slurps her cereal. 'I really, truly do.'

'Well, maybe for your birthday,' says Mum.

'But that's not for a long, long time.' Cleo had her birthday a few days before Christmas.

'You don't get things just because you want them,' says Mum. 'A necklace would be a special present.'

'I really, really, truly, ruly want one.'

Mum rolls her eyes.

'If I don't get a necklace, I'll … I'll …' Words were
stuck in Cleo's throat. Tears were starting at the back
of her eyes. 'I'll be sad for all of my life.'

'Cleopatra Miranda McCann, eat your breakfast.'

On Saturday night, Mum is going out.
Cleo is watching her get dressed. First Mum puts
on a blue dress. She steps into high red sandals.
She pats make-up over her face and puts pink
blush on her cheeks, green eye shadow on her
eyelids and bright-red lipstick on her lips.

'Can I have lipstick too?' says Cleo.

'No way. It's just for big people when they're getting dressed up.'

'I could get dressed up.'

'But you're not going anywhere.'

Mum combs her hair. Then she lifts down her jewellery box. It's made of shiny brown wood and there is a gold lock on it. Cleo reaches out to touch it.

Mum takes out a heavy silver chain but puts it back. She looks at a necklace of brown-and-yellow beads and one made of pale seashells. At last she chooses a gold chain with tiny black stones and slips it around her neck.

'When I get my necklace,' says Cleo, 'it won't have black stones. It's going to have all coloured sparkly ones.'

On Sunday afternoon, Nick comes over.
Cleo and Nick climb up into the tree house and
play shipwrecks. Cleo is the ship's captain and it's
Nick's turn to be the cabin boy. Cleo saves Nick
from a school of sharks and Nick saves Cleo
from a shipload of mean pirates.

Uncle Tom is helping Dad paint
the back fence.

Cleo and Nick climb down from
their ship and lie in the shade
with glasses of icy water.

They watch Dad stirring the green paint in the tin. Then he and Uncle Tom dip in their big brushes and start to slap the paint onto the posts.

It's so hot. Cleo and Nick go inside to get more iced water. Mum gives them watermelon from the fridge. They suck on the slices till they have pink lips and moustaches and then they go outside and see how far they can spit the black seeds onto the grass.

Uncle Tom has taken off his shirt. 'Look.' Nick points at Uncle Tom's arms. Cleo watches as a red-and-green dragon with a spiky back, big claws and smoke coming out its nostrils prowls on the muscles from Uncle Tom's shoulder to his elbow.

A blue dolphin is dancing in the green-and-white waves on his other shoulder. Drops of spray spread up the back of his neck. 'Those tattoos are so cool,' says Nick. 'When I'm big I'm going to get some just like that.'

Cleo has seen them before but today she cannot take her eyes away.

Then she has an idea.

When Nick has gone home
Cleo goes into her room and shuts
the door. She searches her schoolbag
and her toy box and her desk. She looks
under her bed and behind the bookcase.
She finds everything she needs and
starts to work.

After a few minutes, Mum knocks
on the door. 'Are you all right?'

'Yes.'

'Can I come in?'

'No.'

A little while later, Dad knocks on the door.
'What's going on, Cleo?'

'Nothing.'

'Well, dinner is nearly ready.'

'I won't be long.'

Cleo looks at herself in the mirror, grins and
takes off her T-shirt. She puts on her pyjamas.

'Dinner!' calls Dad.

Cleo comes out of her room and into the kitchen. Mum looks at her and raises her eyebrows but says nothing. Dad serves everyone a plate of roast potatoes, ham and salad.

They eat for a few minutes without saying anything.

'What were you doing in your room?' says Dad.

'Nothing.'

'Cleo,' says Mum, 'Dad and I have been thinking. You've been really good lately, so if you really, really want a necklace – if it's so important to you – then maybe we could get you one as a special treat.'

Cleo shakes her head. 'No. It's okay.' She puts down her fork and pulls down the top of her pyjamas. 'You don't have to.'

Around and around her pale neck are lines of
golden texta. Hanging from them are tiny balls
of red and green and tear-shaped drops of blue.
Dots of pink and silver are scattered over the gold.

Cleo grins. 'I've got one already.'

CLeo

and the present

'Pinch and a punch for the first of the month.'

Cleo jumps onto the big bed to wake Mum and Dad.

Dad grabs Cleo's ankle.

'And no return tickets,' she giggles and falls between them.

Mum opens one eye. 'What's so special about September?'

Cleo rolls her eyes. 'It's your birthday,' she says. 'Have you forgotten?'

'Only for a minute,' says Mum. 'But it's brekkie time. Up you get.'

After breakfast, Cleo reaches up to the calendar that is hanging next to the fridge. She counts off the days from September the first to the sixth.

'It's six more days,' she says to Mum. 'What can I give you for your birthday?'

'You don't have to give me anything.'

'Yes, I do.'

'Just be a good girl. You could help
Dad make me a nice dinner.'

Cleo shakes her head.
'That's not a present.
That's not wrapped
up and tied with
a ribbon.'

'We'll talk about it
later,' says Mum.
'You get ready
for school.'

Cleo is walking to school with Dad. She jumps across the joining lines in the footpath.

'Tread on a crack, break your back.'

She stops. 'Dad?'

'Mmm?'

'What can I give Mum for her birthday?'

'What have you thought of so far?'

'Nothing. My brain's as empty as…as…'

'As what?'

'As empty as my shoes are when I take my feet out.'

'That sounds drastic.'

'It's as empty as a garbage bin after the truck comes
and takes everything away.'

'Well, let's fill that empty brain up again.
Why don't you make Mum something?'

'Like what?'

'Why not a painting?
She'd love that.'

'I gave her a painting last birthday. And now I do one every week and she puts them up on the fridge and in her office. They're stuck all over everywhere.'

'True.'

They walk on a bit further. 'I know,' says Dad. 'What about making something from your bead set? You could make her a bangle or a brooch.'

'She never wears things like that.'

'True.'

They reach the school gate. 'We'll talk about it tonight,' says Dad and he kisses the top of her head. 'See ya.'

'See ya,' says Cleo. She runs to join Nick in the lines.

At lunchtime Cleo and Nick play in the dressing-up corner. She is a cat woman and he is a super alien. They sit on the floor and eat Cleo's grapes.

'My mum's having a birthday this weekend. I have to give her something,' she says.

Nick shrugs. 'When it was my mum's birthday, Dad and I gave her a new whizzer for the kitchen.'

'What's that?'

'It chops up all the vegies and you can make soup and even ice-cream.'

Cleo shakes her head. 'That's no good. That would be a present for my dad. He cooks all the dinners in our house.'

That night, Cleo watches Dad chopping the vegies.

'What are you giving Mum for her birthday?' she says.

'Not sure. Maybe a book or a DVD.' He takes a frying pan from the cupboard. 'Do you want to join me? We could give her something from both of us, together.'

Cleo shakes her head. 'I have to give her something from my own self.'

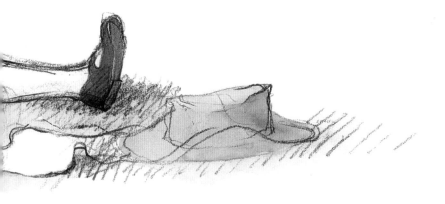

For three days, Cleo thinks hard. Maybe she could use her pocket money to buy Mum something.

She tips up the china pig that she keeps under her bed. Some twenty-cent pieces and a one-dollar coin fall out. Uncle Tom gave her that when she helped him wash his car.

She shakes the pig hard. Nothing more.

She goes to the kitchen and looks at the magazine that comes in the letterbox. It has 'SALE' written across the front in big red letters. Television sets and computers fill the pages. Mum says her computer is an old one but Cleo doesn't have hundreds of dollars to spend.

On the back page there are bottles of perfume
and lots of make-up. Everything costs a fortune.

Uncle Tom comes into the room and looks over
Cleo's shoulder.

'What are you up to, pumpkin?'

'Nothing.' Cleo's shoulders drop.

Uncle Tom ruffles her hair. 'Something's
bugging you. Tell me about it.
Maybe I can help.'

'Mum's birthday is on Sunday and I have to get her a present. And I haven't got a hundred dollars.'

'She doesn't want a present that costs that much money.'

'But I have to get her something.'

'What about making something?'

'That's what Dad said. But I don't know what to make.'

'Put your brain to work. You'll think of something.'

On the day before
Mum's birthday, Cleo finds
Dad in his workshop.

He's fixing the leg of the kitchen stool. Cleo sits on the huge box that the new clothes dryer came in.

'What are you sticking that with?' she says.

'Superglue. It's fantastic. It sticks everything.'

On the bench is a small blue bowl in two pieces. It's the special one that Aunt Jenny gave Mum for Christmas. Cleo knocked it off the table when she was showing Nick how a plastic plate could be a frisbee.

'Are you going to glue that?' says Cleo.

'Not now. I'll do it when I have more time.' Dad leaves the stool resting upside down and he and Cleo go in for lunch.

Later, when Dad has gone to the shops and Mum is busy inside, Cleo goes out into the workshop again. She takes the two pieces of the bowl and pushes them together. They fit perfectly. She can superglue them together, wrap them in birthday paper and tie a ribbon around them. She finds the tube of glue.

It's all crinkled up as if Dad has squeezed it hard many times.

Cleo sits on the floor with the pieces of bowl in her lap. She takes the lid off the tube and squeezes it hard.

Dribbles of glue spread down the broken edge of the bowl. Some runs inside the bowl. Cleo reaches in to wipe it.

Stuck.

Cleo's finger won't move. It is glued hard to the bowl. She drops the tube of glue and scratches at her fingers. Now the pointer finger of her second hand is stuck. She wedges the piece of the bowl tightly between her legs and pulls and pulls.

Nothing happens. Tears are starting to form behind her eyes. What can she do?

Dad always says that no one is allowed in the workshop when he isn't there. What will he say? Cleo gets up and moves to the doorway. What if this glue is so super that it never comes apart?

Never, ever? What if her fingers are stuck like this for the rest of her life and she can't write or draw or wash herself or even wipe her own bottom? How will she hide it from Mum?

She walks slowly back into the kitchen. Mum is at the table, reading the paper. 'What have you got there?' Cleo holds out her hands, stuck inside the piece of the bowl.

Mum reaches out and takes Cleo's hands and the bowl. 'Superglue?'

Cleo nods.

'Was this for me, for my birthday tomorrow?'

Cleo nods again. If she tries to speak she will start to cry.

Mum grins. 'It's not the end of the world. I know something that will fix this.' She disappears up to her room and comes back with a bottle of nail-polish remover. 'This is the one thing that undoes superglue.' She dips a cotton bud into the bottle and dabs at the glue. One by one the fingers come free.

Cleo wipes her cheek with the back of her hand.

Now Mum looks really serious. 'Cleopatra Miranda McCann, no more going into the workshop without Dad. There's too much dangerous stuff in there.' She wags her finger at Cleo. 'And stop worrying about my birthday. I told you, I don't need a present. You are the best present I've ever had, and you always will be. Okay?'

It's Saturday night, the night before Mum's birthday.
At breakfast, Dad will have a present for her. Uncle
Tom will have a present for her. There will be special
food like pineapple and strawberries. Cleo can't
sleep. Even Grandma will have sent a card. She has
to think of something. Then she hears footsteps that
mean Mum and Dad are going to bed. Her eyes
want to close. She has to keep thinking.

And then she has a wonderful idea.

It's Sunday, Mum's birthday.
For breakfast, Dad makes Mum
pancakes with strawberries.

His present to her is on the table,
wrapped and tied up with
ribbon. Cleo is sure that
it is a book.

'My present is still coming.'
Cleo grins.

Later that morning Cleo is in the tree house.
Beside her is every bit of ribbon that she could find.
There are bits for tying up her hair, bits from when
they wrapped presents at Christmas, and even the
bit that tied up Dad's present for Mum.

Carefully, Cleo ties the pieces together to make
one long ribbon. It's not quite long enough,
so she adds the laces from Dad's work boots.

Uncle Tom wanders up to the tree.
'What are you doing, pumpkin?'

'Making Mum's present.
Can you help me?'

'Depends what you want me to do.'

'Go into Dad's workshop and get the big box that's on the floor.'

'Are you going to put something in it?'

Cleo nods.

'Can I ask you what?'

'It's a surprise.'

Cleo has a large piece
of paper. She writes on it:
'To Mum, from Cleo.
Happy Birthday. xxx'

She climbs down and watches
Uncle Tom coming out of the workshop,
dragging the huge box behind him.

He places the box on the grass at the foot of the tree house and Cleo whispers something to him.

Half an hour later, Uncle Tom goes into
the kitchen to find Mum.

'Come outside,' he says. 'Your present from Cleo
is in the backyard.'

Mum and Dad come out together. In the middle of
the grass is the box. The long ribbon is tied around
it and Cleo's card to Mum is stuck down on the top.

'Where is she?' Mum looks up into the tree house.

'She told me to tell you that you are not to wait.
She's giving you the present that you most want,'
says Uncle Tom.

'But she should be here,' says Mum.

'She said you have to open it straight away.'
Uncle Tom's voice is very serious.

Mum frowns and then says, 'Okay. If that's
what she wants.' She steps forward and pulls
the ribbon undone. She tears the card
from the box and the flaps fly open.

Cleo leaps up from inside.
'Happy birthday!' she cries.

First published in 2014

Australian Government

Australia Council
for the Arts

This project has been assisted by the Australian Government through the Australia Council, its arts funding and advisory board.

Allen & Unwin
83 Alexander Street
Crows Nest NSW 2065
Australia
Phone: (61 2) 8425 0100
Email: info@allenandunwin.com
Web: www.allenandunwin.com

A Cataloguing-in-Publication entry is available
from the National Library of Australia
www.trove.nla.gov.au

ISBN 978 1 74331 527 9

Cover and text design by Sandra Nobes
Set in 14.5 pt Horley Old Style by Sandra Nobes
Colour reproduction by Splitting Image, Clayton, Victoria
This book was printed in April 2015 at Hang Tai Printing (Guang Dong) Ltd.,
Xin Cheng Ind Est, Xie Gang Town, Dong Guan, Guang Dong Province, China.

www.libbygleeson.com.au
www.freyablackwood.net

5 7 9 10 8 6 4